# The Big Match

by Damian Harvey and John Lund

FRANKLIN WATTS
LONDON • SYDNEY

Jamal was looking forward to his birthday.

"Only ten more days to go," he said.

Mum was giving Sadiya her breakfast.

"What do you want to do on your birthday,

Jamal?" Mum asked.

Rob was busy washing the dishes.

"Do you have any ideas?" he asked.

"Can my friends come round?" said Jamal.

"We could have a party."

"Only if you don't start running around,"

said Mum. "Sadiya is

only little."

Rob had an idea. "We could all go to the park. You and your friends can have a football party," he said.

"Sadiya loves the park," said Mum.

"And I could make burgers for everyone."

Jamal thought this was a great idea.

He couldn't wait to tell his friends.

When he got to school, Jamal called his friends
over. "Guess what I'm doing for my birthday
this year," he said.

"Are you having a party at your house?"
asked Todd.

"Better than that," said Jamal, grinning from
ear to ear. "I'm having a football party at
the park. Mum says there will be burgers, too."

Jamal's friends cheered. They all thought it was

a great idea.

"Can I come too?" asked Amira.

"As long as you bring me a present,"

laughed Jamal. "Only joking! Of course

you can come."

Later that day, Jamal's Mum got a message on her phone.

"It's your Dad," she told Jamal. "He's got tickets for a big football match on Saturday. He wants you to go with him."

"That sounds great!" said Rob.

"Who's playing?"

"City and United," Jamal told him.

"It's the biggest match of the year."

"That should be good fun," said Mum.

"You love City."

"I know," said Jamal, sadly. "But it's

the same day as my football party."

Jamal didn't know what to do.

"I really want to see Dad

and go to the big match," he said.

"Ok, you do that then," said Mum.

"But I want to play football with

my friends too," said Jamal.

"You can play football in the park with your friends another day," said Rob.

"I know," said Jamal. "But I've told everyone I'm having a football party in the park. They're really looking forward to it."

"What do you think I should do?" Jamal asked.

Rob shook his head. "I don't know," he replied.

"It's up to you. Which one do you want

to do most?"

"I want to do both," said Jamal,

"but there won't be time."

"You will have to make up your own mind," said Mum.

"I know," said Jamal. "But it's really hard to choose."

On Saturday, Jamal was very excited.

"Happy birthday," said Mum, and she gave

Jamal a big present.

He opened it and his eyes lit up.

"City's new football kit!" he cried.

"It's just what I wanted."

"You can wear it this afternoon," said Rob.

At last, Jamal had made up his mind, and now he was looking forward to his party.

That afternoon, Jamal and his friends were

having a great time. Both teams had scored

two goals and the game was almost over.

Then Todd passed the ball to Amira and

she kicked it into the net.

Jamal jumped into the air and cheered.

"Yes!" he shouted. "What a goal!"

"Thanks," grinned Amira, "that was
a really good pass."

"We make a really good team," said Todd.

"And the fans think so too. Look!"

Jamal looked to see where his friend

was pointing.

"Dad!" cried Jamal. "I thought you were going to the big match."

Dad grinned. "This is the only big match that I want to see."

"But what about the City game?" asked Jamal.

"We can go and see them anytime," said Dad.

"Now let's ask your Mum if those burgers are ready."

# Story order

Look at these 5 pictures and captions.
Put the pictures in the right order
to retell the story.

**1**

Dad joins the party!

**2**

Jamal is planning his birthday.

**3**

Jamal can't decide what to do.

**4**

Everyone has fun at the match.

**5**

Jamal gets a new football kit.

# Independent Reading

This series is designed to provide an opportunity for your child to read on their own. These notes are written for you to help your child choose a book and to read it independently.

In school, your child's teacher will often be using reading books which have been banded to support the process of learning to read. Use the book band colour your child is reading in school to help you make a good choice. *The Big Match* is a good choice for children reading at White Band in their classroom to read independently.

The aim of independent reading is to read this book with ease, so that your child enjoys the story and relates it to their own experiences.

## About the book
Jamal is looking forward to his birthday, but he's got a difficult choice to make. Does he have a football party in the park with his friends, or join his dad to see his favoutite team play?

## Before reading
Help your child to learn how to make good choices by asking:
"Why did you choose this book? Why do you think you will enjoy it?"
Look at the cover together and ask: "What sort of event is happening on the front cover? Do you think the boy in the story is going to have to make a choice of some kind? Why?" Remind your child that they can break longer words into syllables or sound out letters to make a word if they get stuck.

Decide together whether your child will read the story independently or read it aloud to you.

## During reading

Remind your child of what they know and what they can do independently. If reading aloud, support your child if they hesitate or ask for help by telling the word. If reading to themselves, remind your child that they can come and ask for your help if stuck.

## After reading

Support comprehension by asking your child to tell you about the story. Use the story order puzzle to encourage your child to retell the story in the right sequence, in their own words. The correct sequence can be found on the next page.

Help your child think about the messages in the book that go beyond the story and ask: : "Why did Jamal have difficulty making a choice about his birthday plans? What did he think about to make a choice?"

Give your child a chance to respond to the story: "Why do you think Jamal chose to have a party? What would you choose to do? Why?"

## Extending learning

Help your child predict other possible outcomes of the story by asking: "If Jamal had chosen to go to the match with his dad, what might have happened? Do you think he made the right decision? Why/why not? Could he have thought of a different solution?"

In the classroom, your child's teacher may be teaching different kinds of sentences. There are many examples in this book that you could look at with your child, including statements, commands, exclamations and questions. Find these together and point out how the end punctuation can help us understand the meaning of the book.

Franklin Watts
First published in Great Britain in 2018
by The Watts Publishing Group

Copyright © The Watts Publishing Group 2018
All rights reserved.

Series Editors: Jackie Hamley and Melanie Palmer
Series Advisors: Dr Sue Bodman and Glen Franklin
Series Designer: Peter Scoulding

A CIP catalogue record for this book is
available from the British Library.

ISBN 978 1 4451 6267 6 (hbk)
ISBN 978 1 4451 6269 0 (pbk)
ISBN 978 1 4451 6268 3 (library ebook)

Printed in China

Franklin Watts
An imprint of
Hachette Children's Group
Part of The Watts Publishing Group
Carmelite House
50 Victoria Embankment
London EC4Y 0DZ

An Hachette UK Company
www.hachette.co.uk

www.franklinwatts.co.uk

**Answer to Story order: 2, 3, 5, 4, 1**